Titles in this series

My book of nursery rhymes
My book of bedtime rhymes
My book of playtime rhymes
My book of animal rhymes
My alphabet book
My counting book
My book of colours and shapes
My book of opposites

British Library Cataloguing in Publication Data
My book of nursery rhymes. — (My square books)
    1. Nursery rhymes, English
    I. Rosenberg, Amye   II. Series
    398'.8   PZ8.3
    ISBN 0-7214-9571-0

First edition

Published by Ladybird Books Ltd Loughborough Leicestershire UK
Ladybird Books Inc Lewiston Maine 04240 USA

Printed in England

My book of
nursery
rhymes

Illustrated by AMYE ROSENBERG

Ladybird Books

Jack and Jill went up the hill
To fetch a pail of water.
Jack fell down and broke his crown,
And Jill came tumbling after.

Humpty Dumpty sat on a wall,
Humpty Dumpty had a great fall;
All the king's horses and all the king's men
Couldn't put Humpty together again.

Little Miss Muffet
Sat on a tuffet,
Eating her curds and whey.
There came a big spider,
Who sat down beside her,
And frightened Miss Muffet away.

Little Boy Blue, come blow your horn,
The sheep's in the meadow, the cow's in the corn.
Where is the boy who looks after the sheep?
He's under a haystack, fast asleep.
Will you wake him? No, not I,
For if I do, he's sure to cry.

Little Bo-Peep has lost her sheep,
And doesn't know where to find them.
Leave them alone, and they'll come home,
Wagging their tails behind them.

Mary had a little lamb,
Its fleece was white as snow;
And everywhere that Mary went,
The lamb was sure to go.

It followed her to school one day,
Which was against the rule;
It made the children laugh and play
To see a lamb at school.

Old Mother Hubbard went to the cupboard
To get her poor dog a bone;
When she got there, the cupboard was bare,
And so the poor dog had none.

Jack Sprat could eat no fat,
His wife could eat no lean;
And so between them both, you see,
They licked the platter clean.

Old King Cole was a merry old soul,
And a merry old soul was he;
He called for his pipe, he called for his bowl,
And he called for his fiddlers three.

I saw a ship a-sailing, a-sailing on the sea,
And oh, but it was laden with pretty things for thee.
There were comfits in the cabin, and apples in the hold;
The sails were made of silk, and the masts were all of gold.
The four and twenty sailors that stood between the decks
Were four and twenty white mice,
   with chains about their necks.
The captain was a duck with a packet on his back,
And when the ship began to move,
   the captain said, "Quack! Quack!"

I had a little nut tree; nothing would it bear
But a silver nutmeg and a golden pear.
The King of Spain's daughter came to visit me,
And all for the sake of my little nut tree.

Mary, Mary, quite contrary,
How does your garden grow?
With silver bells, and cockle shells,
And pretty maids all in a row.

Simple Simon met a pieman going to the fair;
Said Simple Simon to the pieman,
   "Let me taste your ware."
Said the pieman to Simple Simon,
   "Show me first your penny."
Said Simple Simon to the pieman,
   "Indeed, I have not any."

Little Jack Horner
Sat in a corner,
Eating his Christmas pie;
He put in his thumb,
And pulled out a plum,
And said, "What a good boy am I!"

Sing a song of sixpence, a pocket full of rye;
Four and twenty blackbirds baked in a pie.
When the pie was opened, the birds began to sing;
Now wasn't that a dainty dish to set before the king?

The king was in the counting-house,
　counting out his money;
The queen was in the parlour,
　eating bread and honey;
The maid was in the garden,
　hanging out the clothes,
When down came a blackbird
　and snapped off her nose!

There was an old woman who lived in a shoe;
She had so many children she didn't know what to do.
She gave them some broth without any bread,
And scolded them soundly and sent them to bed.

Doctor Foster went to Gloucester
In a shower of rain.
He stepped in a puddle, right up to his middle,
And never went there again.

Rub-a-dub-dub,
Three men in a tub,
And how do you think they got there?
The butcher, the baker,
The candlestick-maker;
They all jumped out of a rotten potato;
'Twas enough to make a man stare.

Jack be nimble,
Jack be quick,
Jack jump over the candlestick.

H ey diddle diddle,
The cat and the fiddle,
The cow jumped over the moon.
The little dog laughed
To see such fun,
And the dish ran away with the spoon.

Little Tommy Tucker
Sings for his supper:
What shall we give him?
White bread and butter.
How shall he cut it
Without a knife?
How will he be married
Without a wife?